ALICE

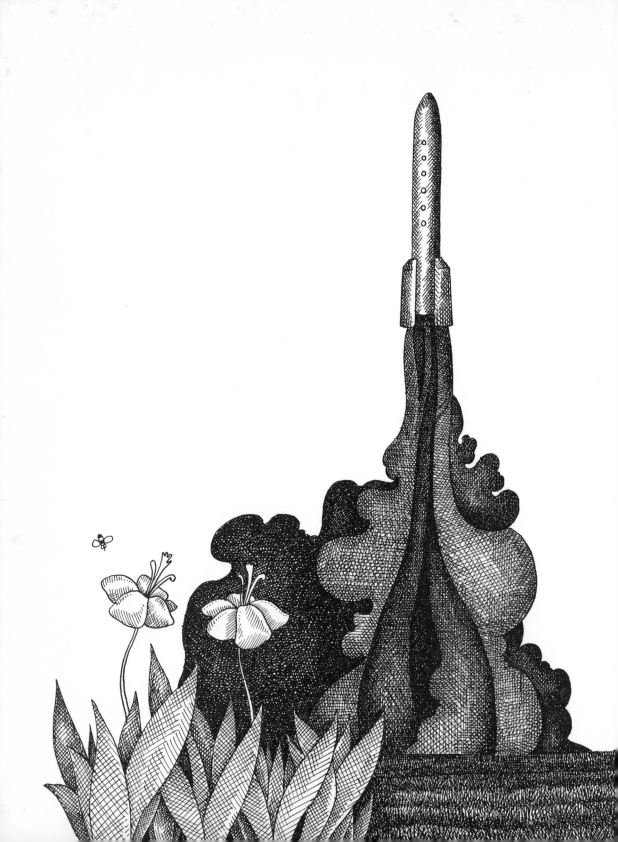

BRONTY

In the beginning, Alice was a child like all children. Until about the age of three. But only a year later, by the time she met Bronty, it was already clear to everyone who knew her that Alice had an extraordinary capacity for doing everything topsy-turvy, getting lost at the most inopportune times, and even making accidental discoveries that astonished the greatest scientists of our time. Alice has many loyal friends, but we, her parents, often find her very difficult—especially because we cannot stay home with her all the time. I am the director of the Moscow zoo, and Alice's mother builds houses, both on Earth and on other planets.

One day the zoo received a gift—a brontosaur egg, found by Chilean tourists in a landslide on the banks of the Yenisey River. The egg was almost round and had been excellently preserved in the eternally frozen Siberian soil. When experts began to study it, they discovered that it was perfectly fresh, and we decided to place it in the zoo incubator.

Hardly anyone believed that the experiment would succeed, but only a week later X-ray pictures showed that the brontosaur embryo was developing. As soon as this was announced, scientists and correspondents flew to Moscow from all over the world. They filled the Venus Hotel, and still there wasn't enough room for everybody. Eight Turkish paleontologists slept in our dining room and bedroom, I moved to the kitchen with a journalist from Ecua-

dor, and Alice shared her room with two women correspondents of the magazine *Women of the Antarctic.*

When Alice's mother videophoned in the evening
from Nucus, where she was building a stadium, she
thought she had reached a wrong number.

All the tele-satellites on Earth showed views of the
egg. They also showed skeletons of brontosaurs.

Everybody wanted to see the egg. But after the first
few days we decided not to admit anyone else to the incubator section, and visitors had to content themselves with
polar bears and Martian praylings.

On the forty-sixth day, the egg quivered. My friend,
Professor Yakata, and I were sitting near the incubator
bubble, drinking tea. We had almost ceased to hope that
anything would hatch. We no longer X-rayed the egg for
fear of harming our "infant," and we could not predict
anything, since no one had ever tried to hatch brontosaurs
before.

The egg quivered again. . . . Then it cracked, split
open, and a black, snakelike head began to push its way
out of the thick, leathery shell. The automatic cameras
clicked busily. I knew that a red light had gone on over the
door of the incubator room. Wild excitement broke out all
over the zoo.

Within five minutes, all those who had to be there, as
well as many who did not, gathered around us. It became
very warm.

Finally, a little baby brontosaur climbed out of the shell.

"Papa, what's his name?" I heard a familiar voice.

"Alice!" I cried out. "How did you get here?"

"I? With the reporters."

"But children aren't allowed here."

"I am allowed. I told everybody I'm your daughter, and they let me in."

I gave up. I didn't have time to take Alice out of the incubator room. And there was no one around who would do it for me.

"Stand there, and be quiet," I said, and rushed to the bubble with the newborn brontosaur.

All of that evening, I was not on speaking terms with Alice. I forbade her to go to the incubator room again, but she said she could not obey me because she felt sorry for Bronty: he might feel lonely without children. On the following day, she was there again. She had been taken in by the cosmonauts from the Jupiter–8 spaceship. They were heroes, and no one could refuse them.

"Good morning, Bronty," she said, approaching the bubble.

The baby brontosaur squinted at her.

"Whose child is this?" Professor Yakata asked sternly.

But Alice is never discouraged.

"You don't like me?" she asked.

"Oh, no, no. Quite the contrary. . . . I simply thought

11

you might have lost your way. . . ." The professor did not know how to speak with little girls.

"All right," said Alice. "I'll go. I'll visit you tomorrow, Bronty."

And indeed Alice came the next day. And almost every day. Everyone became accustomed to her, and no one stopped her. I washed my hands of it.

The brontosaur grew rapidly. In a month, he was nine feet long, and he was transferred to a pavilion built especially for him. He wandered inside his enclosure, munching young bamboo shoots and bananas. The bamboo was brought in freight rockets from India, and the bananas were supplied by a state farm. Warm salt water plashed in a cement pool in the center of the enclosure, and Bronty liked it.

But suddenly he lost his appetite. For three days the bamboo shoots and the bananas remained untouched. On the fourth day, the brontosaur lay down on the bottom of the pool and rested his little black head on the pool's rim. Everything indicated that he was getting ready to die. The best veterinarians and physicians of the world tried to help, but all in vain. Bronty refused grass, vitamins, oranges, milk, everything.

Alice knew nothing about it. I had sent her to visit her grandmother in Vnukovo. But on the fourth day she turned on the television just when the reporter spoke of Bronty's worsening condition. I don't know how she man-

13

aged to get around her grandmother, but that same morning Alice burst into the pavilion.

"Papa," she cried. "How could you have kept this from me? How could you?"

"Later, Alice, later," I said. "We are in conference."

The conference had gone on virtually without interruption for three days.

Alice said nothing and walked away. A moment later I heard someone gasp. Alice climbed over the barrier, slipped down into the enclosure, and ran up to the brontosaur. In her hand she had a roll.

"Eat, Bronty," she said, "or they'll starve you to death here. I'd be sick and tired of bananas too."

Before I had time to reach the barrier, something incredible happened. The brontosaur raised his head, looked at Alice, and carefully took the roll from her hands.

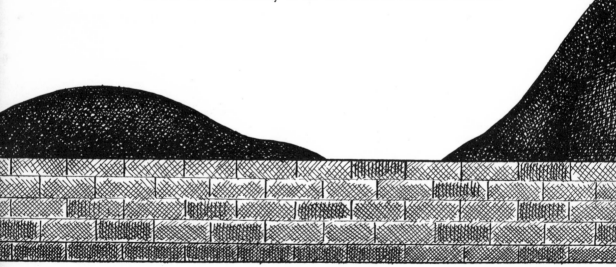

I took Alice with me when I flew to Mars for a scientific conference.

We arrived safely, though I was not very comfortable on the journey. Weightlessness affects me rather badly, and I preferred to remain in my seat. But my daughter flitted merrily about the spaceship, and once I had to pull her off the ceiling of the control room because she had decided to press a red button—the button for an emergency stop.

On Mars, we went sightseeing in the city, joined the tourists on a trip to the desert, and visited the Great Caves. After that I had no more time to look after Alice, and I placed her in a boarding school for a week. Many of our people work on Mars, and the Martians had helped us build a huge atmospheric dome over a children's village. It's very pleasant in the village—real Earth trees grow there. Sometimes the children are taken on excursions outside the dome. They put on little space suits and come out single file into the street.

The nursery teacher told me not to worry. Alice also said, "Don't worry, Papa." And we said good-by for a week.

On the third day Alice disappeared.

It was an altogether unprecedented occurrence. In the whole history of the school, no child had ever disappeared or even gotten lost for more than ten minutes. It was impossible to get lost in the city on Mars. Especially for an Earth child dressed in a space suit. The first Martian who met the child would bring it back. And the robots? And

the Security Service? No, it was impossible to get lost on Mars.

But Alice got lost.

She had been gone two hours when I was called from a meeting and taken to the boarding school in a Martian "jumping jeep." When I appeared, the crowd that had gathered in the schoolyard fell silent in obvious sympathy.

Everyone seemed to be there. All the teachers and robots of the school, ten Martians in space suits (they have to put on space suits when they enter the dome, with its Earth atmosphere), cosmonauts, archeologists, Chief Nazaryan of the Rescue Service . . . .

The city tele-station had been busy for an hour, announcing every three minutes that an Earth girl was missing. All the videophones of Mars were flashing alarm signals. Classes were suspended in all the Martian schools and the children, divided into search parties, were combing the entire city and the surrounding areas.

Alice's disappearance had been discovered when her group returned from an excursion. That had been two hours ago, and her space suit had only a three-hours' supply of oxygen.

Knowing my daughter, I asked whether they had searched every nook and cranny in the school itself and in its neighborhood. She might have found some Martian animal and stopped to observe it.

I was told that there were no basements in the city,

and that every possible nook had been searched by the school children and the Martian University students, who knew every inch of the area.

Reports from search parties poured in: "The students of the Second Martian High School have searched the stadium. Alice isn't there. . . . The Martian Candy Factory reports that no child has been found on its grounds. . . ."

I was getting more and more alarmed. Perhaps she had wandered out into the desert. If she were in the city, she'd have been found by now. But the desert . . . . The Martian deserts hadn't yet been properly explored. You could get lost there, and nobody would find you in ten years. Still, all the nearby areas had already been charted in jumping jeeps. . . .

"They've found her!" shouted a Martian in a blue space suit who was watching a pocket television set.

"Where? How? Where?" excited voices cried from every side.

"In the desert. Two hundred miles from here."

"Two hundred miles?"

"Naturally," I thought. "They don't know Alice. I should have expected something like it."

"The girl is well and will be here soon."

"But how did she get there?"

"In a mail rocket."

"Of course!" said the teacher, bursting into tears. She was more upset than anyone else.

Everybody gathered around her to console her.

"We passed the post office. They were loading the automatic mail rockets. But I paid no attention. You see them a hundred times a day!"

Ten minutes later a Martian pilot brought Alice, and everything was explained.

"I wanted to get the letter," said Alice.

"What letter?"

"You told me, Daddy, that Mama would write us. So I peeked in, to get the letter."

"You climbed in?"

"Well, yes. The door was open, and there were many letters there."

"And then?"

"As soon as I got inside, the door closed and the rocket started. I didn't know how to stop it. There were so many buttons. I pressed the last one, and the rocket went down, and then the door opened. I came out, but there was only sand around. The teacher wasn't there, and the kids weren't."

"She pressed the emergency stop button!" the Martian in the blue suit exclaimed with admiration.

"I cried a little, then I decided to go home."

"How did you know where to go?"

"Well, I climbed a hill to look around, but I couldn't see anything. There was a door in the hill. So I went in and sat down."

"What door?" the Martian wondered. "There's nothing but desert in that region."

"No, there was a door and a room. And a big stone inside the room. Like an Egyptian pyramid, only smaller. You remember, Daddy, you read me a book about Egyptian pyramids."

Alice's announcement caused a great stir among the Martians. Nazaryan, head of the Rescue Service, was especially excited.

"The Tuteks!" they all shouted.

"Where did you find the girl? The exact location!"

Half of the assembled crowd instantly melted away.

The teacher, who took charge of Alice, explained that many thousands of years ago a mysterious people, the Tuteks, had existed on Mars. No traces of it remained except for small stone pyramids. Neither the Martians nor

the archeologists from Earth had ever been able to find a single Tutek structure—only the pyramids, scattered over the desert and half-buried in sand. And now Alice had accidentally stumbled upon a Tutek building.

"You see, you were lucky again," I said. "But anyway, I am taking you back home at once. There you can get lost as much as you wish. And without a space suit."

"I like it better when I get lost at home, too," said Alice.

Two months later I read an article entitled "What the Tuteks Were Like." The article reported that extremely valuable remnants of the Tutek culture had finally been discovered in a Martian desert. Now scientists were busy deciphering the inscriptions in a Tutek building. But the most interesting find was the perfectly preserved image of a Tutek on a pyramid inside the building. A photograph of the Tutek accompanied the text.

The portrait seemed oddly familiar to me. And I was seized by a terrible suspicion.

"Alice," I said as sternly as I could. "Tell me honestly, did you draw anything on the pyramid when you were lost in the desert?"

Before answering, Alice came up and studied the picture in the magazine.

"Yes, that's it. That's your picture, Daddy. But I didn't draw it, I scratched it out with a pebble. I was so lonely there by myself. . . ."

THE SHY SHUSHA

Alice has many animal friends: two kittens; a Martian prayling who lives under her bed and imitates a balalaika at night; a hedgehog who lived with us a short time and then returned to the woods; Bronty, the brontosaur whom Alice visits in the zoo; and, finally, our neighbor's dog Rex, a miniature dachshund of somewhat mixed ancestry.

Another animal joined Alice's menagerie soon after our first expedition returned from Sirius.

Alice met Poroshkov, the leader of the expedition, at a May Day parade. I don't know how she managed it, but she turned up among the children who welcomed the cosmonauts. Imagine my astonishment when I saw Alice on the television screen, running across the square with a bouquet of flowers larger than herself and handing them to Poroshkov himself.

Poroshkov picked Alice up in his arms, they watched the parade together, and left together.

It was already evening when Alice came home with a bulging red pouch in her hands.

"Where were you?"

"Most of the time I was at the nursery," she said.

"And where were you the rest of the time?"

"Oh, we were taken to Red Square."

"And then?"

Alice guessed that I had seen the television program and said, "Well, I was also asked to greet the cosmonauts."

"Who asked you?"

"A friend, you don't know him."

"Alice, have you ever come across the term 'corporal punishment'?"

"I know, that's when kids are spanked. But it happens only in fairy tales."

"I am afraid I'll have to turn the fairy tale into a fact. Why do you always manage to get in where you are not supposed to be?"

Alice was about to become offended when suddenly the red pouch in her hands began to stir.

"And what is that, now?"

"A present from Poroshkov."

"You pestered him into giving you a present?"

"I didn't pester him at all. It's a shusha. Poroshkov brought them from Sirius. A little shusha, a baby one."

And Alice carefully drew from the pouch a tiny six-footed animal resembling a kangaroo. The baby shusha had huge round eyes like a dragonfly. He turned them rapidly, clutching at Alice's dress with his upper pair of paws.

"You see, he loves me already," said Alice. "I'll make a bed for him."

I knew the story of the shushas. Everybody knew the story. We already had five shushas in the zoo, one of them pregnant, and we expected additions to the family any day.

Poroshkov and Bauer had discovered the shushas on

a small planet in the Sirius system. The charming, friendly little beasts who had followed the cosmonauts at every step turned out to be mammals, although in their behavior they were more like our penguins. The same calm curiosity, and constant attempts to climb into the most inappropriate places. One day Bauer had even had to rescue a baby shusha that was about to drown in a large can of condensed milk. The expedition had brought back a long film about the shushas, which was shown with great success in all the motion-picture theaters and videoramas.

Unfortunately, the expedition did not have enough time to observe them properly. The shushas came to the camp every morning and vanished somewhere in the rocks as soon as darkness fell.

Anyway, when the expedition was already on the return flight, Poroshkov discovered three shushas in one of the spaceship's compartments. At first he thought someone had smuggled them into the ship, but everyone denied it so indignantly that Poroshkov decided the shushas must have climbed into the ship and lost their way.

The appearance of the shushas created a number of new problems. To begin with, they could prove to be a source of some unknown infections. Secondly, they could perish on the way, unable to endure weightlessness. Thirdly, no one knew what they ate. . . . And so on.

But all the fears turned out to be groundless. The shushas survived disinfection without any discomfort, and they thrived on a diet of broth and canned fruit. This earned them the bitter enmity of Bauer, who was very fond of fruit dessert and was deprived of his favorite dish because the "rabbits" had eaten it all.

During the long flight a female shusha gave birth to six babies, and the ship arrived on Earth crawling with shushas, big and little. They turned out to be clever little animals and caused no trouble to anyone except Bauer.

I remember the historic moment when the expedition landed and, instead of the cosmonauts, a marvelous six-legged beast appeared in the open hatchway before the assembled crowd and the busy motion-picture and television cameras. It was followed by several other, smaller ones. A gasp of wonder rolled across the earth. But in a moment the smiling Poroshkov followed the shushas out of the ship, carrying in his arms one of the babies, its muzzle smeared with condensed milk.

Some of the animals went to the zoo; others were adopted by the cosmonauts, who had grown very fond of them. Poroshkov's baby shusha ended up with Alice.

The shusha lived in a large basket next to Alice's bed. He ate no meat, slept at night, played with the kittens, and was afraid of the Martian prayling. When Alice stroked him or talked to him, he purred gently.

The shusha grew rapidly, and in two months he was as tall as Alice. They took walks in the park, and Alice never put a collar on him.

"What if he frightens someone?" I asked her.

"He will not frighten anyone. Besides, he'll be offended if I put a collar on him. He is very sensitive."

One night Alice could not fall asleep. She was cranky and wanted me to read to her.

"I have no time, dear," I said. "I have some urgent work. Besides, it's time you started reading books yourself."

"The story I want isn't in a book, it's on a film."

"Well, a film has a soundtrack. Turn on the sound."

"It's too cold to get up."

"Then wait. I'll finish the page, then I will turn it on."

"If you won't do it, I'll ask Shusha."

"Ask him," I said with a smile.

A moment later I heard a soft voice from the next room: "And the good Doctor also had a dog, Avva."

So Alice had gotten up after all, and stretched herself on tiptoe to turn on the switch.

"Go back to bed!" I cried. "You'll get chilled."

"I am in bed."

"You mustn't lie. Who turned on the film?"

"Shusha."

I put aside my work and went to my daughter's room to have a serious talk.

The screen hung on the wall. The shusha was busy regulating the projector, and on the screen the poor sick animals were crowded at the Doctor's door.

"How did you manage to train him?" I asked in amazement.

"I didn't train him. He can do everything himself."

The shusha folded his front paws on his chest, looking embarrassed.

There was an awkward silence.

"Well . . . ," I said after a while.

"Sorry." I heard a high, slightly hoarse voice. It was the shusha speaking. "I really did learn by myself. It isn't difficult, you know."

"Pardon me . . . ," I mumbled. "What I mean is . . . how did you learn to speak?"

"We've had lessons," said Alice.

"I can't understand it. Dozens of zoologists are working with the shushas, and no shusha has ever said a single word."

"Our shusha can read, too. Can't you?"

"A little."

"And he told me so many interesting things. . . ."

"We are great friends, your daughter and I," said the shusha.

"Then why didn't you say anything all this time?"

"He was too shy," Alice answered for the shusha.

ABOUT A
GHOST

We spend our summers in Vnukovo, near Moscow. I usually come there directly from the zoo, but instead of peace and quiet, I am immediately plunged into the turmoil of local life.

Last summer, the population of Vnukovo included Kolya, notorious for appropriating other children's toys; Kolya's grandmother, who was fond of discussing genetics and was writing a book about Mendel; Alice's grandmother; a boy named Yura and his mother, Karma; triplets from down the street who sang in chorus under my window . . . and a ghost.

The ghost lived under the apple tree and was a relatively recent arrival. Only Alice and Kolya's grandmother believed in him. Nobody else did.

One evening I sat with Alice on the terrace, waiting for our new robot to prepare farina for us. The robot had already broken down twice, and we had no kind words for the factory that had produced it. But neither of us felt like cooking, and Alice's grandmother had gone to the theater.

Alice said, "He'll come tonight."

"Who is 'he'?"

"My ghost."

"A ghost is 'it,' not 'he,' " I corrected her, watching the robot.

"All right." Alice refused to argue. "It. And Kolya took the nuts away from the triplets this morning. Why does he always do such things?"

"I don't know. What were you saying about the ghost?"

"He is good."

"Oh, you think everybody is good."

"Except Kolya."

"Very well, except Kolya. If someone brought you a fire-breathing viper, you'd make friends with it, too."

"Probably. Is the viper nice?"

"No one has been able to find out as yet. Its home planet is Mars, and it spits boiling venom."

"They must have offended it. Why did they take it from its home on Mars?"

I had no answer to that. It was the truth. Nobody had asked the viper's opinion when it was brought here. And on the way it had gobbled up the ship's mascot, a dog named Kaluga, which had made all the cosmonauts hate it.

"But what about the ghost? What does it look like?" I changed the subject.

"He walks, but only when it's dark."

"Naturally. That's what ghosts always do. Kolya's grandma has been telling you too many tales."

"Kolya's grandma tells me only about the history of genetics and how mean everybody was to Mendel."

"Incidentally, how does the ghost react to a rooster crowing?"

"He doesn't. Why?"

"Well, a decent ghost is supposed to disappear with

40

frightful curses when the cock crows."

"I'll ask him about it tonight."

"Very well."

"And I'll go to bed a little later. I must have a talk with the ghost."

"Certainly, if you wish. And now, we've had enough of ghosts. Your farina will be overcooked."

Alice sat down to her supper, and I took up an article on the Guiana zoo. There was some fascinating information in it about ukusams. A revolution in zoology. The scientists of Guiana had succeeded in breeding ukusams in captivity. The young were born green, although both parents had blue armor.

The sun set and it turned dark. Alice said, "Well, I'm going."

"Where to?"

"To talk to the ghost. You promised."

"I thought you were joking. But if it's so important for you to run out to the garden, put on a sweater. It's chilly. And don't go any farther than the apple tree."

"Why should I? He's waiting for me there."

Alice ran down into the garden. I turned off the light on the terrace so that I could see her better. She approached the old, branching apple tree and waited.

And then . . . a pale blue shadow separated itself from the tree trunk and moved toward her. The shadow seemed to float in the air, not touching the grass.

41

The next moment, snatching something heavy as I ran, I dashed down the stairs, skipping three steps at a time. I didn't like it. Either it was someone's stupid joke, or . . . . I couldn't think of what the "or" might be.

"Careful, Daddy!" Alice whispered loudly, hearing my steps. "You'll frighten him."

I caught Alice by the hand. The pale blue silhouette before me dissolved in the air.

"What have you done, Daddy? I almost saved him!"

Alice bawled shamefully as I carried her back to the terrace.

What had it been under the apple tree? A hallucination?

"Why did you do it?" Alice wailed. "You promised. . . ."

"I didn't do anything," I said. "There are no ghosts."

"But you saw him yourself. Why are you lying? He cannot stand when the air stirs around him. Don't you see that you must come up to him slowly, so the wind doesn't blow him away?"

I did not know what to say. I knew one thing: as soon as Alice fell asleep, I'd go into the garden with a flashlight and search it.

"And he gave me a letter for you. Now I won't give it to you."

"What letter?"

"I won't give it to you."

A slip of paper was crumpled in her fist. Alice looked at me, I looked at her, and then she gave it to me after all.

The paper was covered with writing—my own notes on the care and feeding of red crumses. I had been looking for the notes for three days.

"Alice, where did you get my notes?"

"The ghost had no paper, so I gave him yours. Look at the back of the page."

On the other side there was a letter in an unfamiliar handwriting, in somewhat stiff language:

Dear Professor,

I take the liberty of writing to you, since I find myself in an extremely awkward situation from which I cannot extricate myself without help. Unfortunately, I am also unable to move beyond a radius of a single yard, the center of which is the apple tree. In my wretched state, I can be seen only in the dark.

Thanks to your daughter, a sensitive, kind being, I have at last succeeded in making contact with the outside world.

I, Professor Kuraki, am the victim of an unsuccessful experiment. I experimented with the transmission of matter over long distances. I succeeded in sending two turkeys and one cat from Tokyo to Paris. They were received in perfect condition by

45

my colleagues. However, on the day when I decided to verify the results on myself, the fuses in my laboratory burned out just at the moment of the experiment and there was insufficient energy for completing the transmission. I was dispersed in space, with the most concentrated portion of me remaining in the area of your esteemed summer home. I have endured this unfortunate condition for almost two weeks, and my colleagues have unquestionably concluded that I perished.

I implore you to send a telegram to Tokyo immediately upon reading this letter. Let someone repair the fuses in the laboratory. Then I shall be able to materialize.

Thanking you in advance, I remain, respectfully,

Professor Kuraki.

I peered into the darkness under the apple tree. Then I went down from the terrace and approached it slowly. A pale-blue, barely discernible glow swayed beside the trunk. When I looked more closely, I distinguished the outline of a man. It seemed to me that the "ghost" raised its arms to the sky imploringly.

I lost no more time. I ran to the railroad station and videophoned Tokyo.

The entire operation took ten minutes.

Gala preparations were in progress to welcome the Labutsilians. The solar system had never yet been visited by guests from such a distant constellation.

The first signals of the Labutsilians were picked up by a station on Pluto, and three days later the Londale radio observatory established contact with them.

The Labutsilians were still far away, but the Moscow Sheremetievo–4 cosmodrome was fully ready to welcome them. Young women from the Red Rose Greenhouse had decorated it with garlands of flowers, and the students of the Advanced Poetry School had prepared a musical and literary entertainment. All embassies reserved places on the special platforms erected for the occasion, and news reporters spent their nights at the cosmodrome restaurants.

Alice was in Vnukovo at that time, and was busy collecting plants for a herbarium. She wanted her collection to be better than Vanya's, who was already in the first grade at school. And this was how it came about that she took no part in the preparations for the festive welcome. In fact, she knew nothing about it.

I did not take part in the preparations, either. My work with the Labutsilians was to begin after they landed.

Meantime, events developed rapidly. On March 8 the Labutsilians reported that they were coming into a circular orbit. Just then a tragic accident occurred. Instead of the Labutsilian spaceship, the tracking station located the Swedish satellite Nobel–29, lost two years earlier. By the time the error was discovered, the Labutsilian ship had disappeared. It was already in the process of landing, and contact with it was temporarily cut off.

On March 9, at 6:33 A.M., the Labutsilians reported that they had landed in the region of 55°20′ northern latitude and 37°40′ eastern longitude according to the terrestrial system of coordinates; in other words, in the vicinity of Moscow.

After that, contact was broken again and could not be reestablished. Earth's radiation had apparently disrupted the instruments of the Labutsilians.

Hundreds of cars and thousands of people rushed to the area where the landing had been reported. The roads were jammed with people searching for the Labutsilians. The Sheremetievo–4 cosmodrome was deserted. Not a single reporter remained in the restaurants. The sky above suburban Moscow buzzed with helicopters, ornitopters, gliders, gyroplanes, windplanes and other flying apparatus. They looked like clouds of huge mosquitoes swarming overhead.

Even if the Labutsilian spaceship had sunk into the ground, it would have been discovered. But it could not be found anywhere.

None of the local residents had seen the ship descend, which was especially odd since nearly everyone in Moscow and its suburbs had been watching the sky during those crucial hours.

There had evidently been some mistake. People were afraid that the visitors might have perished in an accident.

"Perhaps they were made of antimatter," some of my fellow passengers in the suburban train speculated, "and so were destroyed on entering Earth's atmosphere."

"Without a flash? Without a trace? Impossible!"

"Well, how much do we know of the properties of antimatter?"

"In that case, who sent out the message about the landing?"

"Some prankster, maybe."

"A fine prankster! You'll say next that it was a prankster who talked with Pluto, too."

"Maybe they're invisible?"

"The instruments would have located them, anyway. . . ."

Nevertheless, the idea that the Labutsilians were invisible gained more and more adherents.

Later, sitting on the porch, I thought: "What if they landed right nearby, in the neighboring field? And are standing, poor things, by their ship and wondering why people paid them no attention? They may take offense and leave. . . ."

I was just about to go down to the field when I saw a chain of people emerging from the woods, holding hands like a group of children at play. I realized that my neighbors had had the same idea and were hoping to find the invisible guests by touch.

At that moment all the radio stations on Earth broadcast a message that had been caught by an amateur station in north Australia. The message repeated the location of the landing and continued: "We are in the woods. We have sent out the first group of scouts to search for people. We are ready to receive your broadcasts. Astonished at the lack of contact—" At this point the message broke off.

The idea that the guests were invisible immediately gained several million new adherents.

From the porch, I saw the chain of summer residents stop and turn back toward the woods. Just then Alice came up the porch steps with a basket of wild strawberries in her hand.

"Why is everybody running around?" she asked, without greeting me.

"Who is 'everybody'? And you might say hello."

"Hello, Papa. But what happened?"

"The Labutsilians got lost," I said.

"Who are they? I don't know anything about them."

"Nobody does."

"Then how could they get lost?"

"They were coming to visit Earth. They came and got lost."

I felt I was talking nonsense. But it was the truth.

Alice glanced at me with suspicion.

"Do such things happen?"

"No, they don't. Not usually."

"They didn't find the cosmodrome?"

"I guess they didn't."

"Then where did they get lost?"

"Somewhere in the vicinity of Moscow. Perhaps somewhere nearby."

"Are people looking for them in helicopters and on foot?"

"Yes."

"But why don't they come out themselves?"

"They must be waiting for people to find them. After all, this is their first visit to Earth. So they stay near their ship."

Alice was silent awhile, as though content with my answer. She slowly walked across the porch, not letting the little basket with the strawberries out of her hand. Then she asked:

"Are they in a field or in the woods?"

"In the woods."

"How do you know?"

"They said so themselves. Over the radio."

"That's good."

"What's good?"

"That they aren't in the field."

"Why?"

"I was afraid I might have seen them."

"What do you mean?"

"Oh, nothing, I was joking."

I jumped up from my chair. But then, Alice had always had a vivid imagination.

"I didn't go into the woods, Daddy. Honestly, I didn't. That means I didn't see them."

"Alice, tell me everything you know. And no inventions! You saw strange . . . people in the woods?"

"Honestly, I wasn't in the woods."

"All right, then, in a clearing."

"I didn't do anything wrong. And they aren't strange at all."

"Will you give me a straight answer? Whom did you see, and where?"

"Oh, all right. They're here. They came with me."

Involuntarily, I looked around. The porch was empty, aside from Alice, myself, and a grouchy bumblebee.

"Oh, but you're not looking in the right place." Alice sighed and came closer to me. Then she said, "I wanted to keep them for myself. I didn't know everybody was looking for them."

And she held out the basket of wild strawberries. She brought it right up to my face, and, disbelieving my own eyes, I saw two tiny figures in space suits. They were smeared with strawberry juice and both of them sat astride one berry.

"I didn't hurt them," said Alice apologetically. "I thought they were elves out of fairy tales."

But I no longer listened to her. Carefully holding the little basket against my chest, I rushed to the video-phone, thinking that, of course, to our guests from outer space, the field grass must have looked like a tall forest.

That was how we first met the Labutsilians.

A TRIP TO THE PAST

The test of the time machine was to take place in the smaller auditorium of the Science Center. As I picked up Alice in the kindergarten, I realized that I'd be late for the test if I first took her home. Therefore I made her give me a solemn promise to behave and took her with me.

The head of the Time Institute, a very big and very bald man, stood next to the time machine, explaining its construction to the assembled scientists.

"The first test, as you know, was unsuccessful," he said. "The kitten we sent out landed in the early twentieth century and exploded in the area of the Tunguska River, which gave rise to the legend of the Tunguska meteorite. After that we met with no serious difficulties. True, because of certain factors, which you can read about in the pamphlet published by our institute, we are still limited to sending people and objects to the latter part of the twentieth century. Several of our scientists have already been there—naturally, in strict secrecy—and have successfully returned. The procedure of relocation in time is relatively simple, although it has been achieved only after many years of effort by hundreds of people. All it takes is putting on the chronokinetic belt, and . . . . If someone in the audience volunteered, I would demonstrate the process of preparing the traveler for the time journey. . . ."

An awkward silence followed. No one ventured to step forward. And then, naturally, Alice, who had been quiet up to that moment, suddenly appeared on the stage.

"Alice," I shouted. "Come back at once!"

"Don't be alarmed," said the head of the institute. "Nothing will happen to the child."

"Nothing will happen to me, Papa!" said Alice gaily.

There was laughter in the audience, and people turned to look at me.

The lecturer fastened the belt around Alice's waist and attached something like earphones to her ears.

"That's all," he said. "Now she is ready for a journey in time. She needs only to step into the chamber, and she will find herself in the year 1977."

"What is he doing?" flashed through my mind. "Doesn't he realize she'll do just that?"

"Where are you going, child? Stop!" cried the lecturer.

But Alice had already stepped into the chamber and vanished from sight. Everyone gasped.

The head of the institute, pale as a sheet, tried to quiet the noise. I rushed toward him along the aisle. He bent over the microphone and spoke loudly and distinctly:

"The child will not be harmed. In three minutes she will be back in this room. I assure you, the apparatus is entirely reliable. Please don't be alarmed."

It was easy for him to talk. I stood on the stage and thought of the kitten that had turned into the Tunguska meteorite. I both believed and disbelieved the speaker.

"Can I follow her?" I asked.

"No . . . . But please don't worry. She will be met there by our contact."

"You mean, one of your staff is there?"

"No, he's not on our staff. We've simply found a man who has an excellent understanding of our problem. The second chamber is in his apartment. He lives there, in the twentieth century, but in view of his profession . . . ."

At that moment, Alice reappeared in the chamber. She stepped out upon the stage with the air of someone proud of a task well done. Under her arm she had a book.

"You see?" said the head of the institute.

The audience applauded with enthusiasm.

"Tell us, child, what you saw there." The lecturer turned to Alice, barring my way to her.

"It was very interesting," she answered. "Bang!—and I'm suddenly in another room, with a nice man sitting at a desk and writing something. He asked me, 'Are you from the twenty-first century, little girl?' and I said I supposed so, but I never counted our century. I don't count very well yet, I am still in kindergarten. The man said he was very pleased, but I would have to return to my own time. Then he asked, 'Would you like to see what Moscow was like when your grandfather was a child?' I said I would, and he showed me. It was a very strange city, with small, low houses. He told me his name was Arkady, and that he was a writer, and that he wrote science fiction books about the future. But he invented only some of the things in his books; others he learned from people of our century who came to visit him sometimes. Only he couldn't tell anybody about it—it was a big secret. He gave me his book as a present . . . . And then I came back."

The audience applauded wildly.

Then a dignified academician rose from his seat and said, "Little girl, you have a unique and precious volume in your hands. Would you mind giving it to me? You cannot read yet, anyway."

"Oh, no," said Alice. "I'll learn next year, and then I'll read it myself."